The Midnight Hour

By:
Andrea L Wells

ISBN 978-1-5186-4560-0 Paperback
ISBN 978-1-4958-0715-2 eBook
Library of Congress Catalog Card Number:

"There is no friend as loyal as a book."
- Ernest Hemingway

This is dedicated to all my friends -
humans and books.

Contents

"Everything ends in death, everything."
Leo Tolstoy — *War and Peace*

Preface

"So, what's next?" I pressed, trying to recollect

myself as if this had been a part of my plan. I didn't have the

element of surprise but that didn't mean this wouldn't work.

Xavier had surely kept me alive for a reason.

Chapter 1

"This is going to be painful," I mumbled quietly to myself. I knew they were close. I could taste their royal stench on the tip of my tongue.

"Mom, what time do you want me home?" Logan yelled from the top of the stairs.

I choked back a deep sob that rumbled in my chest. Was that the last time I'd hear the sweet sound of my only child calling me *Mom*? Could I really go through with this?

"Come down to the kitchen so we can discuss it, please," I replied, placing my hands on the granite countertop in an attempt to cool my sweaty palms.

I'd spent months, years even, convincing myself that this was the right thing to do that Logan would forgive me. But now that the day had arrived and Xavier was on his way to our home, I wasn't so sure.

Logan stepped around the corner. She was such an intensely gorgeous child. Every parent always thinks their child is the most beautiful person they've ever seen but Logan took my breath away. It all started with her eyes. My own mother used to say, 'the eyes are the window to a person's soul.' If that was the case, Logan's soul was a vibrant teal-blue sea of courage, strength, and a glint of mystery. Her sun-kissed skin accentuated their intensity like that perfect beach shoreline. Her blonde hair, a mix of surely over a thousand golden shades, was pulled up in a tight bun for the evening.

These were all the things the world noticed about Logan at first glance. It was surely what Hollywood was constantly buzzing about, including her perfectly proportioned body. But beneath the glamour, was a being like no one I'd ever met before.

She was our only child; born to two immortal werewolves, and heir to a powerful title – Alpha. Logan didn't know it, but on her eighteenth birthday, she would begin a new life. Her father and I had yet to give her any details.

"Mom?!"

Though startled, I was grateful she called me 'Mom' again. "Sorry," I offered dismissively.

"Brody should be here any minute. What time do you want me home?" she pressed in her best *I'm-a-teenager-trying-to-be-polite* tone.

As she stood impatiently before me, I watched Kevin's perfect smile spread across her face. Her father was devastatingly handsome in a rugged kind of way. His looks, charm, and personality would have made him extremely successful in Hollywood had he come to California with Logan and I. Not for the first time, I regretted that he'd stayed in Wyoming.

"Are Brody's parents' home this evening?" I questioned.

"Why does that matter?" Logan immediately fired back.

I knew Logan was still a virgin and like some teenagers, it bothered her. Hence her edgy-attitude-filled reply. I told her I was proud of her for choosing to wait, which she hated to hear but semi-agreed that it never felt like the right thing to do with Brody. I told her when she found the one, she'd know without a doubt. She rolled her eyes, turned around and walked away – ending that conversation.

Which reminded me of Kevin's attitude – let's not forget about her father's attitude. Kevin was genuinely and patiently kind, but, if provoked, he was stubborn as hell. I could tell Logan was going to be just like him, if not worse, and I was completely okay with that. If she was going to survive as an immortal werewolf, she'd need all of her father's attitude and plenty of my courage to boot. But for now, Logan was just a mild teenage version of him.

"Because if they're home this evening, *Logan*, you may go over to Brody's house after dinner," I replied using my own *I'm-your-mother-don't-push-it* tone. Normally, I would've gotten after her for being sharp with me, but I wasn't about to sabotage these final moments. My heart was beginning to splinter.

The doorbell rang, causing me a panicked jolt.

*There was no way **they** were here yet*, I quickly assured myself. *Nor would they waste their time with a doorbell.*

"Where are you going?" I yelled.

"To get my bag," she said in a rush, taking off up the stairs.

As I turned to open the front door, I let my hand linger on the crystal knob. Our Laguna Beach home was my favorite; Logan's too. Though he had picked the property, Richard was impartial. He never fell head-over-heels in love with anything and that included Logan and I. His priority was real estate, but even with that, he didn't seem emotionally invested. Did he love it? After ten years of marriage, I still wasn't sure. Whenever I tried to talk to him about it, he politely suggested I was too uneducated in the world of realty to ever understand.

Our relationship was founded on business. Richard was the reason Logan and I had careers in Hollywood and we're the reason his real estate business had expanded to celebrity clientele. We've used each other to get to a better place. Did I love him? Sure. He handed Logan and I every opportunity and we wanted for nothing. Did he love me? Sure. He came home to made-from-scratch dinners, a regular rotation of new designer suits, spotlessly kept home, and a warm body to cuddle with occasionally. That is, when he actually *came* home.

I opened the front door not the least bit sorry for neither my marriage to Richard nor my plan to abandon him without warning.

"Hey, Michelle," Brody afforded, forcing a brief smile before he realized I was stopping him at the door. I could faintly hear the sounds of his thoughts questioning, *what my problem was tonight.*

By choice, I hadn't shifted to wolf-form in years. Many years. The last time had been difficult but I awoke one morning to an alien scent: wolf mixed with the sweet scent of pine encompassing our home, the aroma hanging like a smothering cloud. By evening, when I couldn't figure out who or where the scent was coming from, I shifted – barely – hoping to track the intruder down. The trail disappeared at LAX Airport – the international departures entrance – assuring me of one thing – Xavier was continuing to keep tabs on us. Logan was about twelve years old at the time.

Brody played with his BMW key nervously. *I wish Logan would hurry up*, he thought.

Reading Brody's thoughts wasn't difficult, it was how I naturally communicated with shifters when in wolf-form. Unfortunately, if the other person *wasn't* a shifter, then it was a one-sided conversation when in human-form, leaving me with only their thoughts. It was frustrating so I rarely listened to what people were thinking. Since I spent so many years distancing myself from the werewolf world it didn't come as easily anymore. Still, there were a handful of non-shifters I paid minor attention to and Brody was one of them.

Logan was the only exception. I absolutely could not hear her thoughts. To be honest, Logan was *always* the exception.

"I'd like you to take Logan to that new Italian restaurant on Coast Highway… better yet," I paused, realizing I wanted to get her as far away from me and our house as possible for the night. "Take her somewhere nice to eat in Beverly Hills," I said, handing him several crisp one-hundred dollar bills I'd pulled from my Louis Vuitton bag.

"But…" he started, his thoughts quickly coming up with other ways to spend the money he eagerly took from my hand.

"Logan deserves a nice dinner tonight. She's been dealing with some… *things*," I offered cryptically.

I pretended to like Brody for Logan's sake, but I knew he was more than just friends with Logan's best-friend, Lindsey. It was a prime example of telepathy being both a blessing and curse and why I rarely used it. It forced me into an awkward position but I was not about to be the proof-less messenger that typically gets shot in these situations. Did I feel guilty letting my daughter fall deeper in love with a cheater? Of course. But I was absolutely certain Logan and Brody's relationship would end soon and like so many things in life, she'd have to learn the hard way.

Brody tensed at my words, acting as if he wanted to escape. For a young man, he was quite the sight. His career in modeling was extremely promising but until his maturity level caught up with the rest of him, that's all Brody was good for.

"You and I both know Logan deserves nothing short of the best, right Brody?"

He simply and cowardly nodded. *The shit I put up with for this girl,* he thought.

"Then let's not mention this was my idea and you treat her to the best meal in town. I know it's a drive, but she needs this." I gave him my best *you're-not-good-enough-for-my-daughter* smile.

He nodded, acknowledging my unspoken words. At the top of the stairs, I heard the clacking of Logan's favorite black-studded Louboutin heels.

"Hey, Brody," she grinned as she carefully made her way down the stairs.

"Brody," I turned to face him, "would you excuse us for a moment, please? Logan will be out shortly."

"Yeah… sure," he hesitated, looking at Logan. She nodded and he left to start his car.

I took a very deep breath, steadied myself as I shut the front door, and turned toward my baby girl.

"Is everything okay, Mom? You're looking pale."

"I'm just feeling a little off. Maybe I'll head to bed early," I offered, choking back my heart. *Please get through this*, I thought to myself.

"Do you want me to stay home?"

"No, no, no. I'll be fine." *What do I say? What do I possibly say in a moment like this,* I wondered. My heart was starting to shred. I swallowed hard.

"Alright. Well, do you want me home right after dinner? Is Richard gonna be home later?"

This kid, I thought. "No, he's up in Mammoth Mountain area showing a ski property to some new clients. I'll be fine, sweetheart, really." *This can't be it, this can't be it,* I thought.

"Wonderful," she kidded, "Do we know who the celebs are?"

"Umm… he didn't mention it, I'll have to ask him." *That's it, keep it normal and casual. You can do this, Michelle.*

"Alright," she mumbled, reaching to gently squeeze my shoulder. The gesture forced another rumble from my chest and Logan's shimmering teal-blue eyes narrowed in concern.

I grabbed her, pulling her tightly into my arms. I buried my face in her neck, breathing deep. Her designer perfume did little, at least for my nose, to mask the faint scent of wolf hiding beneath the surface of her skin.

I wondered, like I had countless times since her miracle birth, what color her fur would be. I had my assumptions, but was certain she was going to be beautiful and unique in every sense of the word. When thinking about what she was going to look like, I always thought about how she was going to react when she learned of her fate. Thinking about it this time hit me hard because I realized for the first time I would never know. I gripped her tighter.

"I love you, Logan," I whispered softly in her ear.

"I love you too, Mom," she murmured, reciprocating my tight grasp.

I need to let her go.

I pried my face from the crook of her neck, placing a kiss on her cheek. I squeezed my eyes tightly trying to wick away any chance of tears. *This is it*, I thought. My heart was breaking.

Logan pulled back from our embrace. She knew something was wrong, but she'd get nowhere asking. She knew that. Still, the look of concern on her face made my insides turn violently.

"Have fun, I'll miss you," I choked out, nearly losing it.

"I will. Thanks, Mom."

*Ah, **that** was the last time,* I thought painfully. *The last time my heart would ever be whole.*

"Love you," she yelled as she bound down the front steps toward Brody's car.

All I could do as their taillights disappeared down the drive was whisper, '*I love you too*,' as tears poured down my face.

Chapter 2

"Box-color!" I blurted aloud not quite ready to accept the fact that I was alone. "I cannot believe I'm going to dye my own hair with *box-color*."

I starred in the mirror at the mascara-lined tears drying on my cheeks. The lighting in Logan's bathroom made the bags under my eyes look like suitcases – heavy, battered suitcases. I quickly looked away, trying to focus on the hair-color instructions instead. "I have no idea what I'm doing," I mumbled to myself with a smile.

Coloring my hair wasn't necessary, but if I was going to fake my death I needed to do everything possible to ensure my plan worked. It was a plan eleven years in the making, created out of necessity and hinged on hope; one mistake could unravel it entirely.

Eleven years sounds like a long time but when you're raising a child that's racing toward adulthood, even a million years would not be enough. I had been counting down the days, all 4,017 of them, since I made the decision to change both of our lives forever. I knew Xavier would never alter the course of his plan unless I gave him a reason to do so – a reason that made sense. Instead of Logan, I wanted him to take me.

I remember the day Logan was born like it was yesterday. The scene was peaceful and serene. I felt calm. The pain of childbirth was nothing compared to the pain of being born into immortality. And when I heard her gasp for her very first breath, I realized, truly, what love in its purest form was.

She remained swaddled peacefully in the crook of my arm for the rest of the day while Dr. Hanson told Kevin and I the intimate details of Xavier's history. Xavier's parents, also werewolves, had unexpectedly given birth to a son. The only difference: Xavier's mother was already pregnant at the time of her transformation. She screamed out in certainty that she had miscarried when she awoke from her violent transformation in the middle of a bed covered in blood.

Hours later, Xavier was born.

On Xavier's eighteenth birthday, he effortlessly shifted to wolf-form, an unheard of feat – the first shift was often brutal and sometimes deadly. It was immediately apparent something was different about him; the air charged with a new and powerful energy. Within a year, he'd built an empire in London, beginning his reign. He called order to the werewolf world, creating rules to protect, and boundaries to hide our kind. Anything a werewolf could do, he did better. Faster, stronger, smarter in every aspect of what made us unique. Dr. Hanson was certain Logan, only a few hours old, was destined for a very similar path.

I hadn't seen Xavier for close to fifty years at that time, which was a good thing. The only occasion when Xavier showed up unannounced was when that pack, or someone in that pack, had broken a rule. Usually, said broken rule was when a werewolf shifted in front of a non-shifter which meant death for both.

But on that day, no rules had been broken. Instead, the impossible had occurred and the reigning Alpha was coming to witness his potential successor firsthand and worse, try to take Logan back with him to England.

With much tact, Dr. Hanson convinced Xavier she was better off with her parents for the time being. It was then that Xavier, Kevin, and I made our compromise: On Logan's seventeenth birthday, Xavier would return for Logan and she would begin her training with him. Until then, she could live with us. For fear of her telling someone about our world – resulting in her own death – we agreed to not tell Logan we were werewolves nor about her fated future.

However, eleven years ago I changed my mind. While Kevin was hunting with the Callahan's in Arizona, Xavier showed up with Alexander and Raphael to check-in – likely to make sure we hadn't all ran south in an effort to hide Logan. I introduced him to his heir: a five-year old energetic little girl at the time. She was especially hellacious that day and Xavier wanted no part of it. I teased the Alpha pack about what they had to look forward to when she turned seventeen, to which Alexander and Raphael groaned. It was then that I realized they wouldn't want the responsibility of a teenage girl, let alone a newborn werewolf. I began to rethink the arrangement Kevin and I had made.

If it was a strong and confident female shifter that they wanted, I was a willing volunteer.

The alarm on my phone chimed, jolting me back to the cold marble floor I'd been sitting on, waiting for the hair color to process. I checked the time: just after eight o'clock.

"Rinse hair until water runs clear… apply conditioner, leave on for one to two minutes… rinse with warm water… style as usual," I read aloud. "How am I supposed to '*rinse*' my own hair?" I'd always paid someone to touch-up my color but if I was faking my death, it was best I didn't have guests over beforehand.

While I began rinsing away the old me, I tried to listen for Xavier and his pack. Even a more seasoned shifter could usually only hear within a two or three mile radius so unless Xavier was standing on my front porch, it was highly unlikely *I* would hear him before his arrival. These check-ins had become more frequent as we neared Logan's birthday. His arrival wasn't scheduled for a few more weeks.

However. Xavier changed his mind. And when an Alpha changes their mind, *you* change accordingly.

On short notice, I spent the morning preparing for Xavier's arrival while Logan sun-bathed in the backyard. I tried to send her out for lunch so I could attempt shifting for the first time in years, but she had food delivered instead. I gossiped about a huge private sale at our favorite downtown thrift shop, but she wasn't interested. As the hours ticked away, I finally suggested she call Brody for the evening, maybe see a movie or grab dinner. They'd been fighting all week, so it was a desperate shot in the dark that surprisingly worked. The problem was, I never got the chance to practice shifting.

As instructed, I rinsed my hair until the water was clear. Reaching for Logan's shampoo, my stomach immediately twisted into a deep knot, the familiar scent flooding my senses with memories.

My heart began to race painfully at the thought of missing the next few crucial years of her life. Year after year of immortality we would sooner or later cross paths – as long as my plan worked. I didn't know for certain, but it was highly likely I would spend the next several decades confined to The Island.

Once out of the United States, staying out of the Hollywood spotlight would be easier. *But*, once on The Island, no one stood a chance of finding me. In time, I'd be forgotten and could venture back into the world. I hoped.

Kevin and I had only visited Xavier's territory once. If Xavier wasn't interested in visiting you, he sent Alexander and Raphael to fetch you. He made it a point to keep tabs on all packs and when *the* Alpha called for you, you came without protest.

Upon your arrival in London, and depending on whether Xavier wanted to greet you inland or on his island somewhere off the North Sea coast, you were either picked up from Heathrow Airport in a pearl-white Mercedes sedan or were escorted to a black, darkly-tinted helicopter. We were lead to the helicopter.

By the time we boarded, Kevin had to buckle my seatbelt because I was trembling so badly – convinced we had somehow, inadvertently, angered Xavier. Across from us, the Callahan's had the same wild look in their eyes. It took everything I had not to shift, repeating, '*do not shift, do not shift*' like a mantra over-and-over in my mind. By the time we landed, I had no idea where we were or if we'd be able to get back to land if we ran. Steep cliffs of moss covered rock dropped directly into the shore as far as the eye could see.

That's when I realized Xavier was far more gifted than we had ever imagined. He had power to bend the world to his will, the ability to shape his own extravagant kingdom in the middle of the sea.

Though Xavier was forever frozen at the age of eighteen, he embodied authority. Always dapper, he never wore anything less than a tailored, designer three-piece suit – typically Armani these days. Rich, dark brunette hair, toned, tan skin, and his eyes were a piercing shade of bright green. As a wolf, he was menacing: his thick, nearly black fur only accentuating the depth of intensity in his gaze. He was handsome and polished, but also cryptically charismatic and dangerous. One moment, you adored him, wanted to befriend him. The next, he would stab another shifter in the back with a silver dagger, smiling as they dropped to their death.

He was dangerous – extremely dangerous.

And he was about to pay me a visit.

I stepped out of the shower, a foggy haze of heat scattering through the air, and reached for Logan's robe and a towel. It was soothing spending this time alone in her bathroom washing my hair in her shampoo and drying off with her towel. It calmed my nerves as if she was right there coloring her hair with me. I wrapped my hair up tightly in a knot and headed for my closet.

I'd pulled several pieces of my jewelry out of Richard's safe to ensure he got them to Logan. He would do it without realizing it was something I'd planned because he had no idea where I kept all my things, paying little attention to such minor details in his own life. I'd also mixed several pieces in with Logan's own jewelry while she was sunning herself. She'd discover the pieces after she'd moved and settled in with her dad.

I went to the black section of my closet to find an outfit. It had crossed my mind on-and-off throughout the day to pack a bag. No one, not even Logan would notice a bag and clothing missing from my collection, but I finally decided against it.

As I searched through my closet trying to make a decision, my fingers slid across the black fur Gucci coat Richard had bought me one Christmas. Even though Richard had no idea what I really was, I found it so amusing that when I opened the box, I burst into laughter. He became quite upset and long story short, I'd never worn the jacket.

It reminded me again I should practice shifting before Xavier arrived. If anything about my plan started to go horribly wrong, I might need to fight.

I grabbed jet-black Calvin Klein lingerie and set it on the bench beside a pair of new black leather leggings, black Burberry boots, and a plain sheer black tee –aiming to go dark to match my mood. I started to leave the room when I reached back to toss the fur coat on the pile. It would make for a good conversation piece, I suppose.

As I left the closet, I decided my bedroom would be big enough to practice a shift. Plus, I'd be able to watch myself in the oversized mirror. Seasoned werewolves could shift on a dime, but I hadn't shifted for years – there was a chance something might break. An image of Logan shifting flashed through my mind – I knew she was going to look flawless every single time.

I released the towel from atop my head and faced the mirror.

"HOLY CRAP!" I shouted.

I ran toward Logan's bathroom and dove to the floor.

Feverishly shifting through the remnants of the box-color kit,

"…combine color with processor and mix well… Processor?

Which one is the processor? Oh. My…"

There it was. The bottle of processor. Unopened.

I rose to my feet and wiped the condensation from

Logan's mirror with a towel. Wet, golden blonde locks of

hair fell around my pale face. My hair was the exact same

color it had been nearly all my life, not even a shade darker.

Tears began to pool. I'd spent years polishing my plan and

the easiest step had just gone wrong.

This isn't good, this isn't good.

Chapter 3

"What am I going to do?" I mumbled frantically. It was almost nine o'clock, I didn't have any more time.

I slid back onto the cold hard floor. When Xavier informed me he was paying an early visit to check-in on Logan, I feared the worst. He was likely coming to get her, which meant I had one shot to convince him to take me instead. Once she was on The Island, there was no escaping – except by death. This night needed to go perfectly and my hair still being recognizably blonde was not the impression I was aiming for.

"I think I need to go for a swim," I said abruptly.

It was the worst possible time, but I wanted to feel the sand between my toes, inhale the salty Pacific air. Just *one* last time.

I pushed off the marble floor and trotted back to the closet, abandoning my towel. The faint scent of wet dog ever-so-slightly crept into my nose, a smell I never got used to. I grabbed the first bathing suit I could find, black Michael Kors with the tags still attached, and made my way to the second story balcony outside my bedroom.

Our beach frontage was private, but *never* camera free – even if it *was* just our security cameras tonight. As I pulled at the elastic of my suit bottom with one hand, I keyed in the code to our security system with the other, disarming and shutting down Richard's expensive safeguard. I didn't want my late night ocean swim raising any unnecessary questions after I was gone and I certainly didn't want proof of Xavier's visit.

I inhaled sharply just before I dove underwater, slowly letting the air escape my lungs one bubble at a time. For years, I'd thought being immortal meant I was invincible. Then, I bore witness to my first werewolf execution.

In addition to us visiting The Island, Xavier had also sent for a young werewolf from Paris. When our helicopter landed, Raphael whispered something in Xavier's ear and they both stared in our direction, calculating. Xavier finally nodded and motioned for us to follow.

"Please, come," he commanded.

Kevin took my hand as we followed the Alpha Pack toward a garden courtyard. The Island was a twisted mix of magnificent romantic landscape and horrifying medieval architecture, charming rose-lined cobblestone paths and shadowy sinister dungeons.

Thoughts of The Island made my inner wolf rumble toward the surface.

Shackled on either side of the small wooden stage facing each other were a teenage boy and girl. She stared at him in a tormented mix of panic and desperation. He glared at Xavier with a hostility suggesting he was not going to submit easily.

A crowd of lower pack members had gathered and the scent of death and roses hung heavily in the air. Xavier removed his vintage suit jacket and vest, baring his chiseled chest. For a moment, I thought he might be preparing to shift. Instead, he neared the boy.

"You have one minute to explain yourself, Thomas," Xavier announced as he slowly paced back-and-forth on the small wooden stage.

"I have nothing to say to you," Thomas spit.

Xavier coldly smiled and paused toe-to-toe with the boy. "Very well," he grinned forbearingly.

Thomas's eyes bulged, body vibrated as Xavier turned his back on him, searching for Raphael. With a deliberate blink, Raphael shifted nearly on top of the boy as he struggled to shift against his restraints. Alexander stabbed a needle into the boys arm, releasing only a portion of its liquid contents. Thomas instantly weakened and slumped to the floor.

Xavier sauntered to the girl, her beautiful dark blue eyes spilling tears as her body trembled.

"You have one minute to explain," he whispered gently, making a half-hearted attempt to soothe her into confessing.

"Don't tell him anything," the boy slurred.

Her eyes were locked on Xavier's, as if mesmerized.

"I told him I loved him," she whimpered, "…and he wanted to show me something…" Xavier clapped his hands together loudly with a devilish smile, snapping the girl out of her trance and back into reality. She stared at her lover in complete fear.

"But…" she protested.

"I've heard enough," Xavier countered, turning his back on her.

"I'm one of you," she screamed. The scent of her desperation was overwhelming.

Xavier paused, tilting his head to the side. He was no longer smiling.

"I'm one of you," she repeated.

Head still cocked, Xavier pivoted slowly and purposefully toward her.

"He turned me... he's already changed me," she bawled.

I looked at Thomas, his eyes wild with fear, as he fought to rise from the ground.

"He told me if we were going to be together forever, he had to change me. I love him, I'd do anything for him."

Xavier's look of frustration slowly curled back into a menacing smile. "Anything?" he asked.

No! I mentally screamed to myself. Kevin shifted his weight slightly and gave me a knowing glance, silently pleading with me to not make a sound.

"Anything," she answered.

"Well then," Xavier sneered.

He snatched the girl into his embrace, wrapping his hands tightly around her throat, "Die for him," he whispered softly.

I closed my eyes just before I heard her take her last breath. Kevin pulled me tightly against his chest. There was a loud snap, then a dull thud as her body hit the floor.

When I reopened my eyes, the boy was on all fours shaking, face down and slumped over.

"You know the rules," Xavier roared, calling the boy's attention. "Why would you let her stand there and lie to me? She wasn't a werewolf," Xavier spit.

My eyes widened. Kevin squeezed my hand.

"Do you take me for an idiot?" He backhanded the boy across the face with a sharp slap.

Thomas' eyes rose to meet Xavier's. "Yes," he replied defiantly.

"Yes, what?"

"Yes, I take you for an idiot. You're nothing but a coward."

Xavier drew a loaded syringe from his pocket and wrapped his arms tightly around Thomas's weakened body. He growled so quietly in his ear, it would've been easy to miss Xavier's words as he pressed the needle into the boy's neck.

I buried my face in Kevin's chest, choking back a sob, focusing on his uneven breathing.

"I'll never let anyone... anyone, even *him*, hurt you," he murmured softly against my forehead.

I resurfaced from the ocean, gasping for air. Stars glittered across the sky as the dark water rolled with the rhythm of a lullaby. I slowly paddled back to shore, wishing I could crawl into bed and wake up to a normal, peaceful life.

I've never forgotten that day, in Xavier's palace, when I learned we weren't untouchable. Immortality brought agelessness and being a werewolf gave you a very short list of things you could die from. But neither could save you from Xavier.

I needed to call Kevin.

Chapter 4

"Hello?"

I strolled slowly down the shoreline, phone pressed tightly to my ear. "Hey, Kevin," I murmured.

"Michelle! I've been trying to get ahold of you, what's going on? Are you okay?" he pressed.

I hesitated.

"Michelle? I know something is off, I can feel it…" he trailed off.

"I'm… sorry, Kevin," I whispered. My eyes began to water. As soon as I heard his voice, the barriers built around my heart began crashing down.

"Sorry? Sorry for what? Chelle, don't do this to me, what's going on? Is Logan okay?"

"Logan's fine, Kevin. She's perfect."

He sighed deeply, audibly releasing a layer of tension. A *small* layer of tension. "Why are you sorry?" he asked, slightly more calm.

"I'm sorry for everything," I took a deep breath. I needed to confess. If things went wrong, I'd never have another chance. "But most of all, I'm sorry for leaving you."

"Michelle?"

"Let me finish," I began to cry. "You are my soulmate, Kevin Keller. I knew it the moment I met you, I knew it the moment I married you, and I knew it the moment Logan was born. I even knew it the moment we finalized our divorce and I still know it this very second. I'm sorry I waited so long to tell you this, especially after you and I both found someone else, but I need you to know. You've meant everything to me, and I still love you as much as I ever have."

Silence surged between us as I stopped walking. Letting the breeze gently dry my tears, I watched the last slice of twilight dip below the ocean horizon, waiting to hear if he still loved me too.

I heard Kevin inhale deeply. I pressed the phone impossibly closer to my face, desperately wishing he was beside me, that I had done this in person, not waited over a decade to say these things over the phone.

"I know," he whispered softly. "I've always known, Chelle. But, I let you go. I had to. I knew, deep down, you needed this to be happy – I mean, *come on*, we'd been living the same life for over a century, but more importantly, I knew you needed to leave because you thought it would be best for Logan. You were right, she deserved a shot at the closest thing to a *normal* life, even if it would only be for a little while."

I fell to my knees.

"I have and always will love you, Michelle. But, what's going on? Why tell me tonight when I'll be there in just a few weeks for Logan's birthday?"

I took my first easy breath since the day's events began to unfold. He loved me. After everything we'd been through, he still loved me.

Images rapidly flashed through my mind like an old film slideshow:

The day... I met Kevin. I was nineteen, he was

twenty. Kevin's family was in railroad development and my

father was a banker so it was not entirely coincidental we met

at a party downtown. Our fathers were flattering each other

to forge a new business venture together. I could still see

Kevin in the new suit his father made him wear. When we

danced, it complimented my new pale-yellow dress as if

we'd planned it beforehand. Our eyes met and we were

inseparable for the summer as he courted me for marriage.

He introduced me to his friends, including Wyatt Callahan,

and I introduced him to mine, which included Emily

Pinkerton. An inseparable foursome, we all planned our lives

together with our families' blessings.

The day... I married Kevin, July 9, 1865. It was the

same day our best-friends, Wyatt and Emily, were married.

The look Kevin gave me as I walked down the aisle was

inexplicable joy, the look girls dream about.

The day... we struck silver. Our prayers had finally been answered. We purchased our first piece of land, built a home, and a barn – our lives truly seemed to be heading the right direction.

The day... we agreed to be cursed, forever held hostage by immortality. The thought still cools my bones, but even in that tragedy – through the loss of Lance, the many months of deep, dark depression, toxic sickness, and even brushing toward the edge of death, we found comfort in each other, knowing that together there was nothing we couldn't endure.

The day… Logan was born. By God, what a day. She was a welcome surprise and absolutely everything I never knew I wanted. From nearly the moment we become immortal we knew it meant an eternal lifetime *without* children. At the time, the revelation of no children burned me worse than the pain of the transformation. A fire in my soul had been cruelly snubbed out. Over the years, I buried the pain deep and ignored my desire long enough that I could pretend it didn't bother me. I remember our tears of joy when Dr. Hanson had flown in from Italy – Kevin was worried about my well-being – but instead of bad news, we discovered I was expecting our first, and likely only, child.

It was a story, no matter how the evening ended, I'd never get the chance to tell Logan. The slideshow in my mind came to a screeching halt.

"Michelle!?"

Tell him Michelle, he needs to know.

Kevin took a deep breath as if in anticipation.

"Xavier called me. He's decided to come earlier. Tonight."

"Why?"

"He said he's coming to check-in but I think he's getting nervous, worried we might betray him." I paused, knowing Kevin wouldn't like what came next. "He *should* be nervous. That's why I called you, I can't go through with this…"

"Michelle… NO!"

"I'm going to offer myself in exchange for Logan's freedom. I'll join his pack London. Logan can stay with you, Kathrine, and the Callahan boys. I'll promise Xavier that Logan, once changed, will denounce her Alpha status and never lead a pack of her own – you'll see to it. Over time, hopefully, she should lose any special powers she may have had like Xavier because she won't be exercising them. And eventually, Xavier will no longer see her as a threat."

"Michelle, are you out of your mind? He'll kill you. I can't let you do this."

"You can't stop me."

"The hell I can't! Stop and think for a moment!"

"I have thought about it! It's a done deal, Kevin. Xavier will be here soon."

"MICHELLE!" he roared, louder than I'd ever heard him yell in my life. The pure anguish in his voice made me pause and I wondered if I was doing the right thing. But only for a brief moment.

"It's too late, Kevin, I've made up my mind. I knew the day Xavier laid eyes on Logan there was no chance she would be free unless one of us did something."

"What makes you think he'll ever take you over her?"

His point cast a shadow of doubt over my plans.

"I'm his insurance that you'll convince Logan to denounce her status. If you don't, you know what Xavier will do to me. It's a risk I'm willing to take. I'm not afraid of Xavier, I'm not afraid of dying. But I am afraid of doing everything in my power to protect my daughter... and it not being enough."

Kevin was silent.

"We made a deal with Xavier a long time ago, but before that, you and I made a vow to each other. The vow that we'd support each other through thick and thin... for better... or for worse..."

"And you broke those vows, Michelle, when you filed for divorce. Instead of working together like a couple, as a team, you made a decision without me. Then, proceeded to leave me and take my daughter from me. Sure, it may have been the right decision for Logan – to give her a life she deserved for a little while, but it wasn't the right decision for our family. It wasn't the right decision for *us*. Now you're doing it again."

"Don't do this to me, Kevin."

"*You* don't do this to *me*, Michelle. I can't believe you... I can't believe you would do this to me... to us."

"This isn't about you, Kevin. Or me. This is about Logan. It has always been about Logan."

"Exactly!" he growled, "How can you abandon her like this? You're her mother – her best friend – and you're just going to throw that away? I've already lost both of you once, don't do this again. I love her and I still love you."

I sighed deeply – his words stinging my soul. "Love is not always about happy endings."

"You're delusional, Chelle! What do you expect me to tell her? That you ran away with Xavier? You think she won't ever want to come for you, exactly to where you're trying to keep her from?"

"I'm going to fake my own death."

"Damnit, Michelle! I will have NO part in this. I refuse to tell *our* daughter another lie."

"You have to."

"I will not."

I took a deep breath. *This is starting to fall apart,* I thought.

"I'm coming to get you and Logan. Where is she?"

"Kevin..."

The screen on my phone lit up, blinding my left eye momentarily as I pulled the device away from my face.

Dead battery.

That was the end. I wish it had concluded better but I knew the discussion wasn't going anywhere but further and further south. He didn't want me to go through with my plan; I was going through with it anyway. It was ironically nostalgic.

I walked confidently back toward the house, taking a moment to appreciate the perfectly cloudless, star-filled sky again. I was ready.

I knew the risks; I'd gone over every one in my mind but this would work. Xavier was relentless and if we ran, he'd kill us all. If we stayed, he'd take Logan.

I didn't want to leave Logan, I didn't want to fake my death, and I didn't want to walk away from everything I'd ever known.

But what other choice did I have?

Chapter 5

Dear Logan,

This, by far, is the most difficult thing I've ever done because, if you're reading this, it can only mean one thing. I regret putting you through this – no child should have to suffer the loss of a parent at such a young age. But I hope the pain you feel now is temporary and pales in comparison to what could've been a lifetime filled with suffering.

When you were born, you were a miracle beyond measure. I can't begin to describe how much you changed our lives for the better. You were everything I ever wanted and the one thing I feared I would never have – a daughter. Everyone was certain you had a divine destiny awaiting, but I knew they were wrong. Since your birth, you've brought so much joy to not only me, but everyone that meets you. You've matured into a strong and confident young woman whom I'm proud to not only know but call my own. I've tried my best to do everything in my power every single day to care for you, love you, protect you, and above all, to make certain you could choose your own path.

I've always believed that the only true destiny is love.

As you know by now, your father and I

chose to become werewolves – it was either that or die.

Bittersweet because that decision ultimately led me to you

– the absolute love of my life. But it also forever changed

me. I would not change a single, life-altering step, not a

heartbreaking decision, nor a calculated choice. Don't

think, for one moment, that I made any decision because I

had to – I made them because I wanted to. I chose every

path I've been down because of my devotion to you. My

love for you has no bounds.

And love is not always about happy endings.

You were forged from my hopes and dreams

and born from my heart. I leave everything I am with you.

Though the pain of loss never completely fades, there will

come a time when there are no more tears. Trust me, you'll

see. Wherever I am now, I'd rather be anywhere but here

without you.

This is the time, that chapter in your life, when you find out

who you are.

I'll always love you. Far beyond forever.

Love, Mom

Chapter 6

"This is the most prettiest dress I've ever seen,"

Logan declared as she reached her hand up to touch the

violet sequined material.

"Don't do that!" I belted out harshly, instantly

regretting my tone. "Sorry… just… don't touch the dress,

please. This doesn't belong to Mommy, Logan."

"Whose dress is it?" she questioned, her eyes still

lost in the shimmer and sparkle. I pulled her tiny hand away

just before she tried to pick at a shiny sequin.

"It's the designer's dress. Her name is Jenny."

"When's it going to be yours?"

"I don't know, Logan. I don't think it'll ever be mine.

It's one-of-a-kind and far too beautiful for me to own." I'd

begun making a name for myself and with that, more money,

*but I hadn't had my **big** break yet – so I wouldn't be*

affording a dress of this caliber anytime soon.

"You're too beautiful for that dress, Mom."

My heart skipped several beats as a smile beamed across my face. She was so innocent.

"You. Are. Stunning, Michelle!" Jenny offered, barging into the dressing room. "Are you ready to walk?"

"Always."

"I'll be behind you on the runway, so we will cross in the middle. When we get there, let's take a bow together. You and this dress deserve more time in front of the cameras."

"Oh my... are you... I'd be honored!" I squealed.

"Perfect! Then I'll see you out there," Jenny yelled as her assistant pulled her toward a developing disaster on the other side of the room.

"Logan?" my voice immediately escalated in octaves when I turned around and didn't see her.

"Right here," she sang, just a few feet away. Her lips were covered in bright red lipstick, cheeks caked with far too much bronzer and hair pulled up into high ponytail atop her head.

"Logan Leigh Keller!"

"Mom!" she giggled, embarrassed by her full name.

"Don't play with that expensive makeup, it's not yours. Mommy needs to walk the runway in just a few minutes, so I need you to be good while I'm gone, okay? Can you do that for me, please?"

"Fine," she moaned.

"One-minute, Michelle!" my manager yelled.

"Okay, Logan, Mom's gotta go now. I'll be back shortly, alright? I love you."

"I love you too."

I took my first step onto the runway and was immediately swept into the scene. The music momentarily transported me out of motherhood and into modeling. I recognized everyone along the front row as I glanced at them with my peripheral vision, maintaining my stoic gaze. Blinded at the end of the catwalk by all the flashbulbs, I struck a pose and elegantly pivoted. Jenny was walking toward me for the show stopping bow.

As we stood there waving, it was like I'd gone deaf; I couldn't hear a thing. I saw their hands, as they stood in ovation, building what appeared to be a thunderous applause, but the only thing I could hear was the wild pounding of my heart. My vision started to go blurry but I kept waving. I started to feel dizzy. Panic began to take over my body as the energy in the air shifted. I felt my inner wolf bristling, on guard. Just as my smile began to fall from my face, there he was... There. He. Was.

Xavier rose to his feet from the front row at the end of the catwalk, the best seat in the house. His dangerous green eyes, fixated on mine, sent a hard chill racing down my spine. He slowly raised his hands to clap and the moment they connected, the trance broke and I could hear again. A hot sensation shot through me as I froze mid wave.

Beside him, stood Logan.

Chapter 7

The sound of applause jolted me from my lounge chair.

"Good evening, Michelle," Xavier purred as he slapped his hands together with one loud last clap from my balcony door.

"Oh, Xavier! Gosh… you scared me! I must've dozed off after I came back inside. Sorry about that," I offered.

"I have that effect on others," he sneered.

The ocean breeze blew a chill across my skin, carrying his haunting wolf scent.

Behind Xavier, Alexander and Raphael inhaled deeply – likely checking to see if there was anyone else in the home.

"I'm alone," I reassured them, rising to place my novel, *War and Peace*, back on the shelf. It seemed like appropriate reading for a time like this.

"I see," Xavier replied, eyeing the tome with what appeared to be amusement.

Alexander and Raphael split off into different directions to prowl through the house, unconvinced I wasn't hiding a pack of wolves in a closet somewhere. Xavier grabbed my wrist and pulled it forcibly to his lips, gently placing a kiss on the back of my hand. An unwanted shiver raced through me.

"I'm old enough to be your mother," I hissed, pulling my hand away.

"I'm aware," he smiled, "Do you think I'm trying to make a pass at you Mrs. Jarvis?" he teased, releasing a low chuckle from his throat. "I'm just trying to be a proper gentleman. You know, we are from a more civil era, after all."

"It's Mrs. *Keller*-Jarvis," I corrected.

"I've always wondered why you kept Kevin's last name. Still trying to hang onto a love lost?" he questioned.

I wanted to snap, but held my tongue. It would do me no good to be anything but cooperative and pleasant. The sooner I committed to that the better if I wanted them to take me instead of Logan.

"Are you going to invite me in?"

I stepped aside, gesturing for him to enter. Though I couldn't hear his thoughts, I could sense his mood was shifting into Alpha mode. It was an automatic reaction to quickly step into my place below his hierarchy. I couldn't have fought the sensation if I tried; he just wielded that power over lesser shifters.

"Thank you," he grinned. "What a beautiful home you have, Michelle. Where is Mr. Jarvis?"

"Away on business," I replied, sensing he already knew the answer.

"I see. He's away quite often, correct?"

"Yes, he is. Why does that matter?" I countered as politely as I could.

"It doesn't, *really* matter, just curious. But I do still want to know the answer to my original question, 'Why did you keep Kevin's last name?'"

I felt like I wanted to shift. My body vibrated slightly, muscles tightened in anticipation, wanting to pull me into a crouching position. With one hard jerk I believed, maybe, I still had it in me to shift.

"Because," I sighed, fumbling for a reason. "Kevin was my husband for almost one-hundred and fifty years." It sounded like a lousy explanation even to me.

"I see. Do you still *love* him?" he pressed without hesitation.

"Of course," I replied quickly.

"Then why leave him to marry Richard? A *non-immortal*…"

I sighed again. I wasn't sure where his line of questioning was going but I felt the overwhelming push to do as he wanted.

"Kevin and I didn't see eye-to-eye on how to raise Logan," I persisted, wishing I'd just lied.

"And you think Richard has better ideas on how to raise your daughter? Your *soon-to-be-werewolf* daughter?"

"He allowed me to raise Logan the way I wanted to," I explained, yet again, regretting my honesty.

"I see." His simple response was possibly more unnerving than if he had continued to press the issue.

"Do you think he's going to miss Logan when she's gone?" Xavier asked as he made his way through my bedroom and into the hallway, casually inspecting my home.

"Not as much as one might think he should," I replied matter-of-factly.

"And what about Kevin? Do you think Kevin is going to miss Logan?"

I inhaled sharply in response.

Xavier turned to squarely look at me, my face surely tormented with pain. He resumed his stroll, running his hand down the marble fireplace mantle. He stopped at a photograph of Logan and me, pulling it down from the mantle. The day… Logan and I arrived in California. The look on my face said it all: absolutely excited and completely terrified. In my mind, from that very moment on, there was no other option but to be successful with everything I did, including raising my daughter. As her entire life flashed before my eyes, I knew I'd done well.

"Please don't ask me if I'll miss her," I whispered.

"Oh, we both already know the answer to *that* question, Michelle."

I closed my eyes, willing myself to not burst into tears.

"She's grown up since I saw her last," he remarked contemplatively.

I kept my eyes closed, wishing I was still on the beach, toes in the water, and this was just a bad dream.

"Where is our Logan now?"

I finally had enough composure to face him. "She's still *my* Logan, not *ours*," I objected. He was clearly testing me but I had no idea why. I needed to stop letting him provoke me.

"I was looking forward to finally, and formally, meeting the teenage version of her this evening… spending some time getting to know her."

"The house is clear, Xavier," Alexander announced, interrupting Xavier and I standing toe-to-toe in the living room.

I watched a ripple roll through Raphael as he held off shifting, waiting for Xavier to do nothing more than give him a sign to do so.

"Good," Xavier replied, staring me down.

I snatched the photo from his hands, positioning it back in the exact same place next to all her other photographs.

"Shall we?" Xavier asked, gesturing toward the dining room.

A twinge of panic nagged at me and I looked longingly at Logan's photos. I wanted to take them all with me.

Though I knew she'd take advantage and stay out late, there was a small chance she would come home early if she and Brody got into another fight. Xavier would surely take her if she did.

The clock directly above us chimed midnight. Alexander and Raphael both glanced up, slightly in acknowledgment.

"The stroke of midnight, that hour when we're most alive," Xavier began, closing the distance between he and I. "It stirs something in my blood. Immortal, we'll see an infinite number of midnight hours. Its darkness is to us what the dawning light of a new day is to mortals. Our souls may be created with the same set of blue prints," he paused, relishing his own words, "but ours was painted with darkness the moment we were born into immortality."

I stared at Xavier, trying to convince myself his words weren't true. But even after willfully distancing myself from the shifter world, I couldn't disprove a single word. I too felt more alive during the midnight hour than I did the other twenty-three hours of the day.

"I do some of my best work at midnight," he added, sending the hairs on the back of my neck to attention.

"So what prompted this early visit?" I asked, trying to build the courage to offer him my plan. The midnight hour seemed like the opportune time to lay it all on the line.

"I think we need to discuss a few things," Xavier replied, giving Alexander and Raphael a silent indecipherable look.

Is Kevin right? Is this a mistake?

"Very well," I mumbled, as Alexander escorted me toward the dining room.

Xavier and I took seats at opposite ends of the table while Raphael and Alexander closed the doors. I realized, too late, there was no other way out.

Are they trapping me? What's going on?

"Where's the letter you wrote to Logan?" Xavier asked.

I reached down into my pocket with dismay, pausing to look up at Xavier again, "How did you know I wrote Logan a letter?"

A knowing grin spread slowly across Xavier's face.

Oh. My...

"Yes, Michelle, I know your plan, all eleven years in the making."

A warm sensation pricked across my skin, my body began to tremble.

"I'm disappointed, Michelle. Just because you don't care to listen to other's thoughts doesn't mean we all feel the same way. I, for one, have a kingdom to protect. Such a huge oversight on your part.

"And I have to say what you're probably already on the verge of thinking, Kevin was right. *And...* had you listened to him, you and I wouldn't be having this conversation."

I instinctively looked at the guarded doors. *The only way you're coming out of this alive is if someone is on the other side waiting to rescue you.*

Alexander and Raphael both scoffed in amusement.

"So, what's next?" I pressed, trying to recollect myself as if this had been a part of my plan. I didn't have the element of surprise but that didn't mean this wouldn't work. Xavier had surely kept me alive for a reason.

"There is no '*next*' Michelle."

I inhaled sharply, my mind going completely blank.

"This is where it ends," he said matter-of-factly, eyes sparkling with delight as he intently watched me and my plan crumble into pieces.

I stood up quickly, forcing Alexander and Raphael into a crouching position to shift.

"I don't understand," I whispered, "we can still keep our original deal," I pleaded, not trying to hold back the tears that were falling from my eyes.

A devilish grin spread wildly across his face.

The look sent sparks igniting against the warming sensation spreading across my body. I willed myself to shift but nothing happened, the vibration had disappeared.

"The nice thing about being Alpha, Michelle? You can change your mind. You *are* delusional to think that I'd ever let someone as potentially powerful as Logan walk free. I need her and quite frankly she needs us – she needs to be surrounded by pack leaders, Alpha Royalty."

"You're the one that is delusional!" I wailed, "She doesn't *need* you, Xavier. She needs her family. She needs to be with the ones who will protect her and love her. All you want to do is use her for your own personal gains."

"Ha! She "...*needs to be with the ones who will protect her and love her*...?" You've all been lying to her, Michelle. Every single day of her life. Do you really think she's going to want anything to do with you once she learns the truth?"

"Well, do you really think she'll want to come with you after she learns the truth about you?" I countered, knowing a statement like that could mean death for Logan.

"She doesn't have a choice, Michelle. And now, no longer do you."

Everything began to move in slow motion: my breath slowed, my heartrate softened, and my stomach began to deliberately twist and turn. I watched as Xavier deliberately blinked, giving the signal. Alexander and Raphael shifted and for the first time, I saw every detail of their shift gradually unfold – beautiful and captivating. With one hard jerk, their wolf-form ripped through their skin, evaporating any sign of human; clothing fell, shredded, to the floor.

I was paralyzed – my body betraying my mind's only desire: *Shift and run.*

The two wolves growled at either side of me, their hot breath steaming the back of my clenched fists. Xavier stepped in and my knees grew weak as I felt the urge to get down on all fours and bow to his hierarchy: I desperately fought the instinct.

"You're making a mistake," I said with bated breath.

"I don't make mistakes," he replied, taking another step toward me, forcing my need to cower to grow stronger. "I make very concise moves. Quite honestly..." he paused, as if to collect his thoughts, "I never intended on keeping up my end of the deal because I knew you would never keep yours."

"I was... I swear."

"Doubtful. I, of course, wanted nothing to do with raising a child so you won that battle. After nearly seventeen years, I've been more than patient but now my time has come."

"But, she's..."

"Plus," Xavier cut in while casually removing his suit jacket, digging something out of his pocket, "I can't believe you actually thought I'd go for your plan. You're not the one I want, Michelle. I have no use for you."

I released a jagged breath. *This is it.*

Xavier drew a loaded glass syringe into view. The potion was undoubtedly silver death.

Please shift, please shift... My body quivered with grave hesitation.

Xavier snatched me into an embrace, wrapping his arms tightly around my body. I inhaled: sweet pine and damp earth fainted into the background as a new scent came to the surface – blood.

Xavier slowly moved his mouth toward my ear making certain not to loosen his grip as he whispered, "I hope your *'back-up plan'* was making arrangements for your own funeral, Michelle."

I'm sorry, Kevin and Logan, I thought, unable to release the words.

A sharp, stinging pain slowly pierced the base of my neck. My vision went blurry and I instantly started to slide toward the floor. A violent, burning sensation spread like wildfire through my veins. I closed my eyes to stop the spinning, tears spilling over the edge. My body was paralyzed by death, my mind and broken heart trapped inside – a torturous way to die.

This is going to be painful.

Epilogue

"Death is terrible," I read aloud from a dog-eared page of Tolstoy's, *War and Peace.*

I shut my eyes as the rush of adrenaline still coursed through me. My inner wolf snarled and fought to be summoned.

Alexander and Raphael slowly came through the bedroom door and gently laid Michelle's body down atop her bedding. I stepped to the foot of the bed, giving Michelle one final look. She was a remarkably attractive woman: long blonde hair, bright blue eyes, and the perfect bikini body.

"I hate when people dog-ear books," I said, looking at Michelle's closed eyes as I slapped the book shut with one hand and tossed it into the pillow next to her.

"Take care of this so we can leave," I commanded.

"Yes, Xavier," Alexander and Raphael replied in unison. Somedays, I found them annoying, especially after spending decades together. But most days, they proved very noble and useful.

Alpha Guard was their official title, though occasionally they were as useless as pet dogs, they'd spent over three-hundred years serving me well. With the rise of werewolf witch trials sweeping London in the late 16th century, Alexander and Raphael were desperate to gain control needing something greater than them to turn things around. Befriending an elderly widow whom they knew was actively practicing witchcraft; she taught them how to create the ultimate alpha. Weeks passed while they constructed the perfect plan until they happened upon my father and pregnant mother enjoying one last stroll near Hyde Park. A few days later, I was born and I've been stuck with these *guards* ever since.

"Here," I said, handing Raphael the chemical solution to flush Michelle's system of silver. "Make sure you test her blood before we leave. Her death will **not** go unnoticed. Take anything we need to destroy including her cellphone."

Folklore was *almost* correct, the only way to kill a werewolf was with silver. But it was too often messy. So, several hundred years ago, I'd asked Dr. Hanson to develop a cleaner and more effective method: liquid silver. When autopsies became more popular, I tasked him to invent a mixture to flush out the evidence. 'Cause of death' was an important lie to maintain if I wanted to protect our kind. Dr. Hanson was brilliant, even if he wasn't thrilled about using his inventiveness to grant criminals' death warrants. A loyal subordinate, he never vocalized a word of his disagreement to me. Neither did most shifters.

I closed my eyes, paused briefly to bid Michelle farewell, and left the room without a backward glance.

Somber violin music drifted quietly through the house speakers as I studied the photo-lined walls down the hallway. I vaguely knew about Michelle and Logan's celebrity lifestyles, but I had no idea of its depth – a depth that was going to make my next move more difficult.

Though the justification she gave for divorcing Kevin was not entirely true, she at least made the right decision in moving to Hollywood – it suited her. She'd clearly made quite the life for herself.

I strolled further down the hallway to Logan's bedroom. Her sweet, floral perfume was something I could easily get used to, though, it did very little to mask her lingering dog scent. It had been several hours since she last set foot in her room which meant she could be anywhere in California by now.

Admiring her photos, I briefly thought of Logan as a potential mate. What wasn't to like about her: exquisite thick golden hair, mesmerizing eyes, slender body, and legs that went on for days. And though I hadn't spent more than a few brief moments with her since she was born, I knew she was strong-willed, confident, and intelligent – a natural-born leader. I've dated hundreds of girls but none like Logan. To be honest, Logan could be my exact type – a perfect and my only true match. However appealing the idea, there was a crucial deal breaker: I wanted nothing to do with the female werewolf side of her, or any mate for that matter.

Unwelcome thoughts of Sienna broke my train of thought. Several decades ago, I broke my own rule and dated a werewolf. She was wild - edgy, and beautiful in every sense of the word: short black hair, pale-green eyes, and a body that every girl was jealous over. She was and still is extremely fashion-forward, even taking up modeling for a few years. But, Sienna never committed to anything for too long, enjoying the fact that immortality afforded her the luxury of living many lives. It was a fundamental difference between us that I shouldn't have ignored.

In the beginning, she loved that I was Alpha – I was her latest hobby. But she's a lone wolf at heart. I pushed the unbidden thought of her aside – I was content dating non-shifters. Historically, they were easier to come by and took less effort. When they started planning our future together, I ended it – permanently. On our very last date and in the throes of passion, I'd bite their neck, scarring them for life. I may not age, but they do – if I ever saw them again, I wanted to steer clear.

Are we going after Logan? Raphael thought, clearly getting restless to access the beast within and hunt.

Just worry about Michelle right now, I replied.

I'm sure she's not far, probably still around L.A. It wouldn't take us long to track her from that restaurant, Alexander offered.

Or, we could wait for her here… let her see Michelle dead in her own bed… then drag Logan with us back to The Island… Raphael thought.

Focus on one thing at a time! I instructed, then shut them back out. I could filter my thoughts so they could only hear what I wanted. It was something only I could do. There were a lot of things only *I* could do. Logan Keller could change that.

I continued to stroll around her room, running my hands across her things – searching for something but no idea what.

Dr. Hanson was certain she was fated to be just as powerful, if not more so, than I. Michelle was foolish to think I'd ever let Logan roam free. I may have had no interest in raising a child but now old enough she would prove to be either an asset or an adversary.

My phone began vibrating from the depths of my coat pocket. It was the call I'd been expecting.

"What can I do for you, Kevin?" I asked as I placed the phone against my ear.

"What have you done?" he breathed.

"Kevin, I'm sorry for your loss. I think you already knew this was coming."

He took a slow deep breath, swallowing his grief. "Where is Logan?"

"I have no idea and I think you already knew that Logan wasn't here. If she was, you and I both know I wouldn't have answered your call."

He said nothing, likely in agreement.

"I'm also fairly certain Michelle purposely didn't tell you where Logan was going this evening so you would have nothing to hide from me. You know… it's surprising to me you had no idea Michelle spent the last decade scheming behind your back."

"If you're trying to insinuate I knew…"

"I haven't said such a thing, just making an observation."

"Had I known, tonight would have never happened," he asserted.

"Fair enough."

"So let's get on with it, Xavier," Kevin sighed. "Where do we go from here and what about our original arrangement?"

"Well..."

"Please, my daughter is going to need me now more than ever in her lifetime. She needs to be in Wyoming with me. Michelle may have broken your trust, but I have not and you know that. Let's be fair, though I don't like it and my heart is now completely broken, I can understand why tonight happened. There's a right way and a wrong way to go about doing something and Michelle clearly made a mistake. I think, given the chance, we could've solved this problem differently," he paused, swallowing hard. "She was a wonderful woman and only trying to protect her daughter. I was betrayed too, and I'm angry too, but give *me* the chance to work the rest of this... situation out," he insisted.

I had always admired Kevin. He was well-respected among other shifters, something I was not. But, he also never had to make the types of decisions I was faced with. Still, he was maintaining his decency and integrity and it would serve no good to punish that type of loyalty.

"I agree, Kevin. You have not betrayed *my* trust and I have no reason to betray yours. Our arrangement stands. But I'm warning you, if anything, *anything*, goes awry... our deal is off."

I hung up the phone. The man likely needed to grieve.

"We're finished," Alexander announced as he and Raphael entered Logan's room. "Want me to see if I can pick up Logan's trail..."

"...even though you told Kevin we weren't?" Raphael finished eagerly.

"I'm a man of my word," I snarled, stepping directly before them. They both visibly flinched, resisting the urge to cower. "End of discussion."

Raphael's eyes flashed wildly in disappointment.

"I'll allow Logan to go back to Wyoming to be with her father. When the time is right, we'll go collect. If anything goes wrong or they resist for any reason, we kill them."

"What about the Callahan's?" Raphael interjected, "I've never liked any of them."

"You just don't like the fact that our plan didn't work when they refused to join the Alpha Guard after their parents died," Alexander countered.

"They won't cause trouble under Kevin's watch –he's a man of his word," I interrupted. "You two will take turns checking-in. Alexander – stay here and keep an eye on Logan. Make sure she's safely delivered to her father after the funeral."

I started to leave Logan's room when I noticed a large frame with several photographs of her with a younger man.

"Who is this?" I asked, pointing at his face. He was clearly someone with celebrity status, but I'd never seen him before.

"That's Brody Wilson, Logan's boyfriend," Alexander replied.

He was well-built and seemed attractive; paired up nicely with Logan.

"Are they serious? How long have they been together?" I pressed, annoyed. Alexander and Raphael were supposed to keep me informed – they hadn't so much as mentioned this.

"I'm not sure how long, but from what I can tell, they're serious enough – puppy love." Alexander replied.

"Hmmm," I breathed as I began carefully opening the picture frame and removed one of the photos. "This could be useful."

"Logan's probably with Brody now. Do you want us to go find him?" Raphael asked, cutting into my train of thought.

"No," I replied sternly, my mind silently swirled with new possibilities.

"Our plane is ready," Alexander said, hanging up his phone as I looked up from the photograph.

"Go get me Rachel," I commanded.

Acknowledgments

Thank you to my best friend and husband, Travis. I wouldn't
be where I am if not for your unwavering love and support.
I love you.

Thank you to my son, Ty, for keeping your sister, Katie, busy
while I write.
Thank you to my daughter, Katie, for keeping your brother
busy.
I love you both so ridiculously much.

Thank you to my friend, Christina Fifer. This book would
have never hit the page had it not been for your commitment
to me and my passion.
I appreciate you.

Thank you to the design genius, Amanda of
PixelMischiefDesign.com. You are extremely supportive and
exceptionally brilliant.
I can never thank you enough for both.

Thank you to the family and friends who have been so
seriously supportive of this journey.
I value each and every one of you.

And last but absolutely not least, thank you to my fans, my
readers, my followers, and every single book blogger I have
the pleasure of now calling a friend.
The Midnight Hour is for you.

25555557R00059

Made in the USA
San Bernardino, CA
03 November 2015